I0838235

FRAGMENTS OF THE AFROVERSE

FRAGMENTS OF THE AFROVERSE

100-WORD STORIES

RAN WALKER

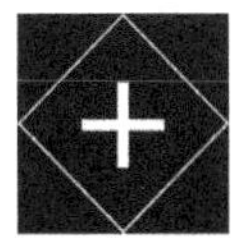

BLACK + SQUARE PAPERBACK EDITION

© *2025 Randolph Walker, Jr.*

All rights reserved. Published in the United States by Black + Square, LLC.

No part of this book may be reproduced in any form or by any electronic or mechanical means, including information storage and retrieval systems, without written permission from the author, except for the use of brief quotations in a book review.

Cover photo courtesy of Story Zangu
Cover Design by Randolph Walker, Jr.

ISBN: 978-1-961753-18-1 (Paperback)
ISBN: 978-1-961753-19-8 (Ebook)

First Edition
10 9 8 7 6 5 4 3 2

Black + Square, LLC
Hampton, VA

Contents

PART TWO
MIDNIGHT

PART THREE
SHADOW

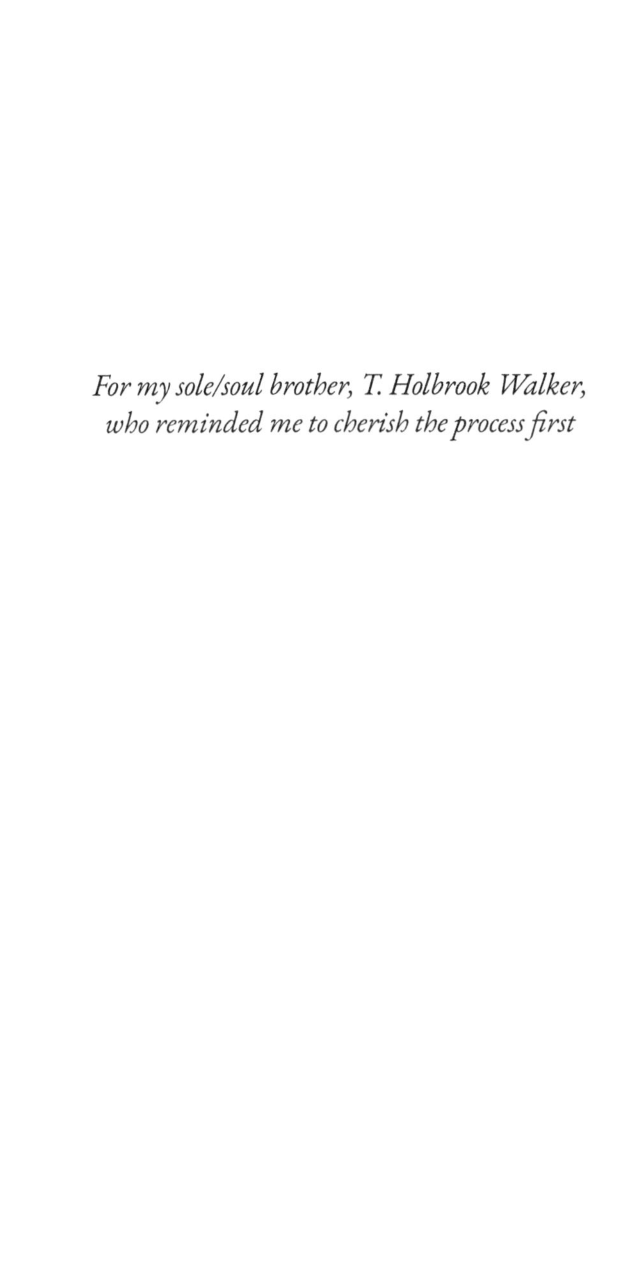

For my sole/soul brother, T. Holbrook Walker,
who reminded me to cherish the process first

The biggest nation is the imagination.

— RZA

Part One
Veil

Fragments of the Afroverse

Around midnight, there's a new puzzle piece on my windowsill. No notes. No box. Just a shape that feels familiar when I hold it.

Some tabs feel like places I've dreamed of. Others feel like memories I had forgotten. I don't know who's sending them, but I keep putting them together, each piece changing something.

Yesterday, the mirror blinked. Today, my little brother floated for five seconds before hitting the floor, laughing.

Grandma says I'm building the Afroverse. Says it's been waiting on me. I don't know what happens when it's done.

But I'm almost there.

I can feel it.

THE END OF RIVERTON DRIVE

AFTER SHEL SILVERSTEIN

The morning after Little Charlotte Townsend's birthday party, the residents of the Riverton Drive cut-de-sac awoke to find an enormous, dead blue whale lying in the street, blocking them in their driveways.

The Townsends wondered openly about how it got there. The Jacksons complained it would make them late for work. The Smiths worried about the pending scent of decay becoming unbearable. The Taylor's teenage daughters took videos of it and posted them to social media.

Finally, Little Charlotte emerged, fork and knife in hand, and said, "Shel* said we should eat it one bite at a time."

---

* Shel Silverstein is the author of *Where the Sidewalk Ends*, a collection of children's poems that includes the poem "Melinda Mae."

Love on a Plate

She delighted in cooking for him. This was how she expressed her love. She regularly served him fine meals she'd discovered online and cooked to perfection. She even sought out more exotic meats, feeling the more difficult it was to secure an ingredient, the more she loved him.

He ate each meal, oftentimes complaining about a lack of seasoning or a texture that simply felt "gross" in his mouth. He didn't see these meals as anything special, definitely not acts of love.

Since he wouldn't give her his heart, she carved it out, broiled it, and served it to herself.

UGLY

She hadn't noticed that her fingers had grown longer, her nails thicker. It was only when her boyfriend commented on the hairs on her back that she took notice. Once she realized what she was becoming, she refused to leave her penthouse.

For years, she'd insulted the celebrities she'd interviewed, dragged their personal struggles through the city streets for the entertainment of her listeners and the resulting ad revenue.

Now, she had become the subject of gossip and rumors, some saying she had transformed into some strange beast, as if the ugliness of her words had become manifest in flesh.

CHARLOTTE DAY'S NECKLACE

The kids at school openly pondered if the bones on the necklace around Charlotte Day's neck were in fact real. That debate quickly gave way to what type of animal the bones could have come from. Were they from the bones of a pet who had died?

As the day progressed, so did the darkness of the students' theories. Maybe they were human bones. Perhaps an uncle had severed a finger or two in some type of lumberjack accident. Some even wondered if they were the bones of a child.

Finally, they asked Charlotte, whose only response was a smile.

Chicken

She sprinkled salt and pepper on him as he slept, and when he finally sneezed and awakened himself, he asked what she was doing.

"Salt and pepper. Salt and pepper. We could have won that competition if only you'd used salt and pepper on the chicken!"

He sat up in his bed irritated, then brushed himself off. "You were right there next to me. You saw me adding the salt and pepper!"

"But it wasn't enough."

"It never is," he responded.

"Yes, it is. You just under-seasoned the food!"

"So you're seasoning me?"

"What else would you do to chicken?"

I'd Rather Die Alone

It wasn't the idea of dying in an accident that Garrett feared; it was the idea of dying in an accident alongside his twin brother, Gregory. Gregory was the one who had all the talent. He was the one who had gone to college on a drama scholarship and been cast in a box-office hit upon graduation. He was the one who was a three-time Oscar nominee (having won twice). He was the one who received $35 million for his last film (even though it tanked). If Garrett died next to him, he'd be a footnote in his brother's obituary.

Be Careful Not to Fall to the Bottom

She cannot shake the thought of her classmate falling into a sinkhole that was apparently beneath his bedroom. At her age, she will obsess over this, trying to imagine his last thoughts as he plunged to his death so unexpectedly. This was not a suicide or car accident or an athlete succumbing to heatstroke in the swelter of summer. (She would wrestle with those, but at least she could understand that those things, though unfortunate, happen in high school.) But this creeped her out on an entirely different level. It placed everything upon a platform that felt far too fragile.

THE WHITE VAN

The boys couldn't know for sure if Mr. Townsend was a pedophile, kidnapper, or murderer, but he looked like one to them —or so they convinced themselves.

Mr. Townsend drove the customary white van, which he parked on the corner of Elm, down the street from Dr. Mae C. Jemison Elementary School. No one knew what he did for a living, but one of the boys had called him "creepy," and adjectives like that stuck to a person like heavy-duty wallpaper.

As they beat him with hammers and bats behind his white van, they convinced themselves they were administering justice.

The Latchkey Kid

Tasha carried the key around her neck, on a thin rope that she kept beneath her t-shirt, against her training bra. Her mother didn't get home until after five, and she'd convinced her mother she was responsible enough to keep herself out of trouble for an hour and a half. She could make herself a sandwich and do her homework.

Still, she would sometimes see a man in a white van across the street from her apartment building, looking in her direction when she got home.

She prayed he would never knock on her door, and he never did.

Screaming

She was practicing her scream.

One couldn't always expect a scream to do what it should (startle, alert, or warn), so learning how to open one's mouth, pull from the diaphragm, as her music teacher had said, reach for the highest decibels of sound, and allow that chaotic orphan of cacophony to sail, unobstructed, through the air beyond her breath, could not be something that merely happened, instinctively or involuntarily.

It had to be cultivated, as a vintner might a fine grape. It had to be perfect for when the monsters eventually came.

Her scream had to save her life.

Camera Obscura

My doppelgänger is upside down, but we are joined like a face card in a deck. He is me, and I am him, and we mirror each other, twins across intersecting multiverses, the sun blazing against my back, the moon against his, and we move in tandem, our voices like echos, and I begin to lose myself to this "us," this tethered self that refuses to let go, no different that I, as there is comfort in this connection because neither of us is alone. We live and die like Chang and Eng,[*] for we cannot live without the other.

---

[*] Chang and Eng were conjoined twins (the original "Siamese Twins"), who had a career doing sideshows, including those run by P. T. Barnum.

Horror, My Ass

Joshua sits in the theater, exasperated at what was supposed to be a horror movie, but it is not. Most of them aren't. Dark suspense maybe, but definitely not horror. He doesn't know if it's marketing or laziness on the part of a studio that doesn't really know its movie all that well. Having aliens, vampires, zombies, ghosts, or doppelgängers in a movie doesn't make a story automatically horror in nature, but he has come to accept that expanding (or altering the definition) of a word is en vogue these days. If you label it that, that's what it'll be.

Returning to the Area Code of the Commercial

She'd been too clever. She now understood this. She had tangoed with the language, hips sliding, shoulders carrying a tight wire, and she'd lost them, her readers, somewhere over the abyss of her stories. She'd kept pushing both her stories and readers too far. She realized she'd been writing for herself—its own private delight— but that was not what she needed to survive in the publishing industry. After all, one did not conceive by masturbating. There should, ideally, be a con- sensual exchange between two parties: her and the reader, so she reluctantly decided to dial it back a bit.

I Contain Multitudes

She positioned the camera on a tripod and pointed it at herself. At first the poses were serious, mouth sealed in the style of the 19th-century models, teeth sealed behind pursed lips, but that was not her. She tried smiling, Cheshire grin eating her face like Pac-Man chomping a ghost, but that, too, felt fake.

Then she stuck out her tongue, a playful gesture that seemed to ignore the camera. Moments later she imaged hands around her neck, closed an eye, and gritted her teeth. She did this until she eventually grew tired.

Among those photos was the real her.

A Place Called "15 Minutes"

The banks just didn't get it. Neither did the investors.

Lease a few homes. Lease a few luxury goods. Get a few interns to scream (if screaming was what the customer wanted) or fawn over the customers, smart phones in tow. There would be a red carpet (of course). Maybe some caviar and fancy cheeses. Prop money for those who enjoyed gaudiness. The key was to make the customer feel famous, not necessarily rich, so as long as they were seen in this way by others, nothing else mattered.

Andy Warhol was right, and she was determined to prove it.

The Love Poem That Refused to Die

Alexander began his poem while he was studying literature at Morehouse, some fifteen years ago. It began with one muse, but over that time the poem had taken on many muses. He has not yet completed the poem, though, believing that there is something greater to say with this idea, which now spills over three hundred pages (and counting), but now he is locked between the present and the glue of what he knows is nostalgia staring at him from those pages. He must admit to himself that the poem is no longer about love, but his infatuation with it.

You Will Not Get Me

In her dreams, there is a man in white latex gloves, and he is reaching for her neck. He wants to squeeze the life from her. She's knows this just like she knows the best way to pick plantains. It is instinctive.

What *he* doesn't know is that she will not go easily—even in a dream—and that she will fight him with all that she has. She will pull back each of his meaty fingers, one by one, peel the skin from them like plantains, and bite into them with her hungry mouth until they are no more.

Jamar Meets the World

When Mr. Hardy informed Jamar that he would be held back in 9th grade for the third time, Jamar simply shrugged. He tried to imagine a future where what he learned in school played any role in his life. If it ever came to that, he would get his GED, which he'd heard wasn't all that difficult these days. His plan was to take on odd jobs and travel the world. Maybe he would learn a trade or something, but he refused to sit up in Mr. Hardy's classroom yet another year, watching more younger kids make him feel stupid.

Flower Boy

The other boys had caught Lawrence by surprise. He was seated, legs crossed, hands probing the soft soil, the petals of Black-Eyed Susans dancing against his shoulders like the sun's fingertips.

Why are you out here messing around with flowers? they'd asked.

He made up some lie about a girl in their grade, one that none of them pined after but that he figured they would begrudge him a crush anyway, and the fact he was picking her a bouquet to get a kiss.

Kisses being the currency they were, the boys soon left him alone to enjoy the flowers.

BLACK TRUMPET

The trumpet is beautiful: a matte black, trimmed in brass. It looks like its owner loves it. It is not merely an instrument lugged into a band hall to be blown by someone with poor embouchure, who leaks spit on the guy's foot next to him. No, this instrument was meant to be played on magnificent stages in front of paying audiences or at festivals in Copenhagen, Montreal, or New Orleans. Its owner likely attended Juilliard or Berklee and views music as transcendent—a religion. She longs to be near it and receive its message when it is finally played.

1986

That summer they rewatched Val Kilmer build lasers and John Cusack ski on one leg, kid-wasted off Slush Puppies that were mixed with every flavor (which they playfully called "suicides"). They rode their bicycles through town, the sun shining on their shoulders. Maybe they'd stop by the public library, still high off of *Reading Rainbow*, wanting to escape everything for a little while. At night, they'd sit on the porch, staring out into the sky, while people occasionally walked by waving, the crickets getting worked up, the scent of a grill down the street, and the deep sleep that followed.

One Afternoon in Dr. Milton's Waiting Room

The two men sat across from each other in the waiting room, at first content to keep to themselves. Finally, the older of the two men spoke up.

"It's the shoulder," he said, trying to rotate it. "Been bothering me something awful."

The other man, now beginning to relax, responded, "Maybe it's not as bad as it seems."

"Yeah. Maybe," the older man responded. "What are you here for?"

The second guy paused before answering. "Just getting my routine physical."

"Prostate this year?"

"Yep."

The older man laughed. "Well, I should probably warn you that Dr. Milton has big fingers!"

Homework

When he makes it home before curfew, he lies in his bed, the lights turned out, Bobby Brown's "Roni" playing softly in the background, and stares at his ceiling, thinking about her. He's never dated a senior, but she has found him (a sophomore) to be more desirable than her peers.

He is remembering her kisses and how it felt when she let him touch her. He thinks to himself that everything about her was wet, and while he never thought he would crave wetness, it is now all he can think about.

He gets up and locks his door.

A Hero's Lamentation

Zaria sometimes dreams all of her classmates are lined on either side of the bus lane in front of Octavia E. Butler Middle School. They are creating a runway of sorts. She then begins to run as fast as she can, until her feet lift from the ground, hover for a moment, then push her into the vast sky, where she glides like a golden eagle over her small town. Feeling the cool wind rushing against her face, she closes her eyes, wishing this was her superpower, but it is not.

Zaria must instead settle for her gift of invisibility.

PART TWO
MIDNIGHT

The King James Version

Alice Mosley had been threatening to retire for years, but at the last minute, she'd always found a way to push it off. She continually saw more that she could do, more ground that she could cover, a higher elevation at which she could plant her final flag. In her mind, she considered herself the greatest of all time when it came to doing her job, and whether anyone else agreed, she was not even concerned in the slightest. She had done it longer than anyone else, and, subsequently, she'd accomplished more, so she would retire when she saw fit.

Protect Ya Neck

We took our places in the theater, five rows from the stage, when the guy from the couple behind us began to sneeze. It wasn't a loud obnoxious sneeze, nor was it a soft whimper, but it was *wet*, as if he was spraying a mist of mucus and saliva across the crook of his arm into the backs of our seats. He sneezed again three more times in rapid succession, the mist racing towards our necks, as we cowered in our seats. Meanwhile, his partner echoed "Bless you," but this nicety couldn't undo the germ monster building behind us.

Octogenarians Talking Smack

She'd always whispered her observations of others to him, most of them colorful remarks that in their younger days he might have found funny. Now, approaching 80, neither heard as well, so her whispers fell on deaf ears, literally, with her husband nearly yelling in response, the way one might do if talking over music in a set of headphones.

"You said what?! He looks like someone beat him down with an ugly stick?!"

She could hear him but was too embarrassed to respond. She knew she shouldn't talk about people, but old habits died hard—or not at all.

THE MIRACLE
WE ARE

Shortly after the singer passed away, many of her fans gathered at the iron gates outside her mansion and laid bouquets and pictures on the ground. Although she had recorded over twelve albums, the mourning crowd instinctively knew to sing "The Miracle We Are," a lesser known recording from her third album, as it seemed the perfect song to exalt her legacy, like "Man in the Mirror" or "Imagine." It was also one of the few songs she had recorded during her lifetime that she had actually written, a song that would soon become her biggest contribution to the world.

It's a Sneaker Thing (You Wouldn't Understand)

DaMarcus is afraid to admit to his mother just how much he spent on his sneakers. He doubts she would understand that they were a limited edition collaboration between a popular rapper (of whom he owns none of the rapper's music) and a brand notorious, not only for releasing hype footwear, but also for dropping limited pairs using elaborate stunts like scavenger hunts that take sneakerheads through the city, where they board buses and travel to pop-up stores at leased bodegas in distant neighborhoods.

DeMarcus knows he could flip the sneakers and make a killing, but he'd rather wear them.

HER VOICE

They joked about her voice, how low it was, how *husky* is was. They said it sounded like she'd been smoking cigarettes since she was six, that she gargled with rocks instead of mouthwash. They talked about how she was the female version of that character Froggy from *The Little Rascals* (even though only two of them truly understood that reference). One guy had even said she needed to walk round with another girl to talk while she lip-synced.

None of them expected her singing voice to be so powerful or that they'd end up apologizing through their overwhelmed emotions.

DEEP CUTS

There is a generation of viewers that goes through art with a fine-toothed comb, pointing out the subliminals in a K.Dot diss tracks or the hidden elements in a Childish Gambino video or the Tarantino references in *The Vince Staple Show's* season finale, not realizing writers have been doing this all along, these deep allusions that skate past the casual reader but serve as a wink for those who appreciate deep cuts, this beckoning forth of a memory that better informs the present and allows them to experience the magic over and over again, with different results each time.

Baloney

Marlon stared at the baloney in the skillet, watching it bow until it became a crispy meat bowl. His cousin had told him to slit the sides, but he wanted the meat to be perfect. Now it had curled and cupped itself into a meat toy. He no longer wanted to eat it, but he couldn't deny his hunger.

His cousin handed him the bread, a butter knife, and jar of mustard. He took it reluctantly.

As he tried to flatten the baloney on the bread, he asked, "What's in baloney?"

His cousin shrugged. "Some things are better left unsaid."

CRACK KILLS

When Aaron turned 45, he noticed that his body cracked in more places than it ever had. He was used to being able to pop his shoulders and lower back, even his knees, knuckles, and big toe, but now everything was starting to pop. If he looked too quickly to either side, his neck cracked. When he reached over to tie his shoes, his arms and back sounded like a Gatling gun.

He wondered if this would worsen as he grew older. This couldn't continue indefinitely. What if one day he discovered he could pop himself into a million pieces?

Sleepless

He stares at the ceiling, counting everything that is countable, thinking that if he exhausts himself enough he will finally fall asleep. He puts on soporific audio books and even a podcast where some guy rambles about random things, while a rain shower pours down in the background. He changes positions, stacks and unstacks pillows, drinks warm milk, pops melatonin tablets, and even polishes the banister, but nothing works. He stares at the ceiling, his furrowed brow creasing the darkness.

He will continue to lie in bed, his mind racing, never realizing that he has been asleep the entire time.

Lost Shadows

Chloe didn't notice it at night, because everything is a shadow, but when the sun sailed above her on that July summer afternoon and she looked down, she realized there was nothing there, nothing that echoed her form, nothing that would provide shade for tiny creatures. No matter how she rotated her small body in the sunlight, no shadow appeared on the pavement. Not even her fingers, formed into the shape of a giant bird, cast a shadow next to her Mary Janes. Maybe she was invisible, she considered, or maybe she was transparent and light simply passed through her.

CAMILLE'S RECITAL

Camille plays piano in the empty hall. Her fingers strike keys that produce no sound, yet the air vibrates with familiar sorrow. The audience of ancestors watches, mouths still, eyes aglow. Each note births a flicker of light that dissolves before reaching the ceiling.

Camille plays the piece she's never learned but somehow knows, and the room breathes with her, expanding and contracting. When she finishes, the familiar silence returns.

The ancestors fade, satisfied. Outside, dawn births magenta along the horizon. She takes one last look at the piano, and smiles. This has been her greatest performance yet, she realizes.

Black Flower Stains

Every morning, Andre spills his coffee at exactly 7:25. The stain blooms like a black flower on his shirt. He changes it, leaves for work, returns, then sleeps. The next day is no different, nor the day after that. Once, he skipped his coffee entirely, but the stain still appeared, as precise as before. The calendar on his phone never changes. Even his neighbor waves in perfect rhythm each morning., and the birds sing the same wrong note.

He wonders if he's trapped inside a loop, or if the loop has become him. Either way, the stain always returns.

The Never-ending Haircut

Malik has been getting his hair cut for the past decade. He's never left the seat, and all day and night he hears clippers buzz, hands glide, the mirror refusing to reflect any progress. Mr. Purnell hums an old tune, lost in a memory—of what, Malik hasn't the slightest.

Malik's phone rings again, the same call from the same number. More hair falls like snowflakes into similar patterns on the floor. He wants to leave, but he's stuck in this chair, his haircut in a perpetual state of happening.

Mr. Purnell smiles faintly. "Almost done," he says.

Always *almost*.

The Door to Anywhere

Charlene is the first of the three girls to notice the door standing in the middle of the playground. She has heard of doors like this, doors that lead to other dimensions. If her brother was around, he would probably tell her that it was a bad idea to open the door and walk across the threshold—but he is no longer there. He is buried within her mother's grief and Charlene's loneliness. She considers the other three girls and what they might do but knows deep down she doesn't care. The choice is hers, as it has always been.

Music You Can Grow Old To

Xavier's parents told him rap music wouldn't last, that it was just a fad for people who couldn't sing, that, at its best, it was people reading poems, and at its worst, it was just noise. Now, as he takes his teenage sons over to see their grandparents, his father remarks about Kendrick Lamar winning a Pulitzer Prize for *DAMN.*, while claiming that *good kid, m.A.A.d city* is still his favorite of K.Dot's joints. His mother points out that Doechii's paying homage to Minnie Riperton on the cover of *Alligator Bites Never Heal* slaps.

Go figure.

Dreams of a Poet

Zora came across the vintage leather trunk suitcase while combing through a thrift shop in Little Five Points. Something in it captured her imagination, and she immediately took it home and laid it open on the floor of her bedroom. The plan was to use this suitcase as motivation for saving for and taking that trip to Paris she'd always talked about. She had plans to sit at a table outside of Shakespeare & Company, journaling in a black notebook with a fountain pen. The suitcase seemed like a symbol from the universe, but sadly, it remained empty, a dream deferred.

Don't Call It Smut

Every night, Julian dims his e-reader's glow, angling it just so—safe from judging eyes, even in the privacy of his room. He devours sentences like stolen kisses, heart racing not from the stories, but from shame. He dreams of writing his own: bold, aching, soaked in longing. But what would his friends say? His colleagues? The whisper of scandal permeates like perfume. Still, he scribbles lines in secret notebooks, hiding them. Each word feels like a confession. *One day*, he thinks. *Maybe*. But for now, desire lives in shadows—between paragraphs and in the silence after the last page.

THE CYBORG

You scoured the alley for shattered radios and the discarded bones of machines. You gathered them like offerings to the future self you hoped to become. In your room, you welded silence into shape: a soda can elbow, a copper spine, steel plates wrapped around tender calves. The metal burned, but you welcomed its truth. Humanity had become a sickness—loud, cruel, unbearably soft.

Robots didn't bleed.

Robots didn't ache.

Your voice began humming, low and hollow, your pulse thinning to an echo. At dinner, your mother stirred soup, unaware of the shimmer rising up your throat, transformation nearly complete.

Just Once

The world darkened a little more each morning. Edges softened and colors faded like old denim. Carl ran his fingers over photographs, trying to remember textures, not images: his wife's gentle smile, the wonder in his daughter's eyes. *Soon*, the doctor had said. The light would go.

He sat by the window, watching their garden blur into a wash of green and brown, trying to hold the picture in his mind. But it was the child he hadn't met that haunted him.

His grandson.

Not yet born.

Please, he whispered to the sky, *let me see him once. Just once.*

THE BACKPACK

Dion walked with stories stitched into his backpack. Words hummed like soft drums on his spine. At school, the noise cut deep—side-eyes, laughter, names that stung. When it got too loud, he slipped to the corner, unzipped the pack, and crawled inside. The hallway faded. There, gods welcomed him with nods. Aunties with wings served sweet thunder. Boys like him soared through cities made of light and jazz.

He read, flew, and healed, as time outside held its breath. When he returned, eyes clearer, hands steadier, no one believed a thing.

But his backpack was still warm, still humming.

We Made a Movie Once

During the summer of '84, they found a busted VHS camcorder at a yard sale—ten dollars and no charger. They filmed everything: kung fu fights in alleyways, love scenes on stoops, chase scenes through sprinklers. No script. Just sweat, laughter, and light. What started out as a joke became something else—raw, weird, beautiful. A film stitched from Black boy joy and sistas who knew how to direct better than anyone gave them credit for. Years later, some made real movies, budgets and crews, but none of it felt like that summer—when they made something out of nothing.

Mixtapes Aren't Forever

While her kids played in their bedrooms, she found the cassette in a box buried beneath old *Ebony* and *Jet* magazines. No case. Just a handwritten label: *For You*. He'd give it to her at a time when everything felt urgent, like love might end the world. She held it, tried to remember the songs—Aaliyah, Maxwell—but nothing stuck. Just echoes. That love had been loud, messy, full of almosts. Now, her life moved to a steadier beat. A husband who stayed. Kids who needed lunch. She walked to the trash, dropped the tape in, and never looked back.

THE MONARCH

Lashonda told the witch she wanted to be a monarch butterfly, to fly and be free of rules and voices telling her what she couldn't do. The witch nodded, whispered something softly, then made it happen.

Lashonda opened her wings, and the wind carried her. For the first time, she felt weightless.

Then she learned the truth—monarchs don't live long. Maybe a few weeks.

She begged to change the wish, but the witch shook her head. "You got your wish."

So the girl kept flying, the sky too wide to turn back. Beauty, she understood, could be cruel, too.

A Record of
His Life

Pops always said he wrote *that* song—the one Jimmy Ray, a white man with slick hair and blue eyes, turned into a fortune.

"He took my story," Pops growled, "my pain."

Before Pops died, he made one last request: press his ashes into a vinyl of the song *he* wrote. The family reluctantly agreed.

Pop's voice trembled from the speakers—raw, righteous. Then Ava, three and wild, knocked it from the turntable, and it shattered.

Silence.

Ava giggled.

Outside, Jimmy Ray played on the radio, but now, they only heard Pops—and that broken silence felt more like truth.

PART THREE
SHADOW

Two Things Can Be True at Once

Dennis woke to find Victoria staring at him, her smile crooked and unsettling. The bedsheet had slid down to her bare hips, and the sweet softness of her breasts lay before him, as if being served. He'd fantasized about being here in this moment with her: waking up to her beauty and enjoying another round (or two) before breakfast. But her smile was off-putting. Something wasn't quite right. For a moment he had a flashing thought of the horror franchise *Smile*.

"Is everything okay?" he asked, steeling himself.

"It is now."

This was what he'd wished for, he reminded himself.

Marooned

Antoine's arms ache and his legs are beginning to cramp, but he continues to tread water. He is alone with ocean for miles in every direction. No one knows he is here. His makeshift boat is floating debris that is too far out of reach at this point. Maybe he should have stayed on the island and lived out his days eating fish and coconuts and drinking collected rain, but he felt he had to at least try to get back to civilization. Now, he is adrift with only his thoughts and a dark, unforgiving sky looking down on him.

THE RELUCTANT AQUANAUT

Vanessa has figured that it is more advantageous to be an aquanaut than an astronaut. The billionaires have commodified trips out of the atmosphere, and everything out there, assuming you could get to it, has to be terraformed. The water, however, is easier to comprehend. It is the more affordable option. But there is no less science involved: understanding water pressure calculations, maintaining a proper breathing apparatus, merely seeing more than a few feet in front of you. It is not ideal, but then neither is strapping yourself to a rocket. Some people can afford a choice, but Vanessa can't.

Playing Catch in the Street

Marvin can barely remember his childhood friend throwing the football to him, as he ran from light pole to light pole. He just remembers his feet gracing the asphalt in quick spaces, the ball hitting his hand and forearm, and the celebratory yell of his friend from several yards away.

They hadn't spoken in years, so news of his friend's death hits him differently. He is left to wonder all of the life that was lived after their childhoods and how he'd missed it. This is how he must mourn his friend: a childhood wrapped in a collection of memories.

MOTHERHOOD

Eileen dozed off in the nursery, the lullaby still humming in her throat. Warmth enveloped her like a blanket, as the rocking chair creaked. When she awoke, the air felt different, older. The crib was gone. In its place stood a man with familiar eyes. He smiled with the same crooked dimple she had once kissed goodnight.

"Mom?" he asked, his voice deep.

Eileen glanced down at the wrinkles now lining her hands, wrinkles she hadn't earned. She reached out to him, hands trembling.

He held her gently, like something sacred.

"You were just..." she whispered.

"I know," he said.

Central Park Mall

Daysia lies in the shade of an American Elm, its canopy far above her head. The sounds of the city vibrate beneath the Azymuth playing in her AirPods. Central Park is animated with beautiful people of all shapes, colors, and ages, and she feels in this moment that this is where she belongs. Her cells are screaming at her that she is a New Yorker at heart. This place is nothing like Tuscaloosa, Alabama, or Jackson, Mississippi, or even Atlanta, Georgia. Here she feels free of labels. Here she feels *free*.

She closes her eyes and hums a Brazillian melody.

An Ode to Regina

Alex composed the song for her, hoping to play it for her one day and impress her, hopefully make her see him as more than a friend.

One day while hanging out at her house, he noticed her piano sitting in the living room. Elementary sheet music rested in the stand.

"Are you learning to play?" he asked her.

"Yes."

"Can you play me something?"

She obliged, struggling to get through the sheet music.

Afterwards, he asked if he could play a song he wrote for her.

Taking it as him trying to embarrass her, she reluctantly agreed to listen.

Skunk

J ared carried with him the funk of someone who'd been hotboxing before class. He claimed it was his roommate and the scent must have gotten into his clothes.

One of his classmates smiled. "Just take half a gummy."

Another classmate said, "Man, don't do that. They don't measure it out right."

A third classmate told him that vaping might help but that he had to be careful because of the studies.

The professor cleared his throat. "Are we ready to begin class?"

They all nodded and focused their attention on the cybersecurity PowerPoint.

Jared sniffed himself, trying to smell anything.

FINDING MY WAY
BACK TO YOU

They had married at a cobblestone church on a small hill in Atlanta and had gone on to have two girls, who were now in college at Howard and Spelman. They owned a house in a haughty subdivision in PG County, but more than anything, they loved each other madly.

But she doesn't know any of this now.

He made the mistake of walking through a door that took him back in time 25 years.

He has just met her for the first time and is desperately trying not to scare her with the future he hopes still awaits them.

Bones

Or Speaking Music

Torrance walks around with the mouthpiece of his trombone in his back pocket. If he could carry the trombone itself everywhere, at all times of the day, he would walk around playing it as if it were his primary form of communication.

The band hall, though, is his sanctuary. Still, he cannot live in the band hall, so he carries this mouthpiece, this silver-colored piece that can unlock the secrets of any trombone or baritone, sometimes holding it in his hand like a metal cigarette, ready to place it against the sweet spot of his lips and speak music.

KISSING JAZMINE

All year, Carter watched Jazmine, with her sunlit hair and easy laugh, floating through the halls of Windsor High School. When she finally said yes to grabbing lunch, he nearly forgot how to speak. Afterward, sitting on a bench in the park, she leaned in, his heart jackhammering like crazy.

Their lips met—and clashed. Teeth bumped. Her nose squished awkwardly into his.

She pulled back, laughing, cheeks flaming. "I'm... really bad at this," she mumbled.

"Me too." He grinned.

They tried again, slower. Still clumsy, but warmer this time. Maybe beauty wasn't about perfection after all. Neither was love.

Black to the Past

Miles sits in the theater watching movie trailers of period pieces from the early 20th century, movies where, if they were being completely authentic, they wouldn't have a single Black person in the cast, but because the film is being released in 2025, the casting director has taken some liberties and hired a few Black actors to stand around passively in the background, completely divorced from the mores of that time period. Miles believes it's good for there to be diversity in movies, but when Black people are used as some kind of anachronistic backdrop, he'd rather not see it.

BONES
OR LEARNING TO LOVE YOURSELF

Marilyn wants to look like the thinnest women in fashion magazines, so she decides to skip meals each day and eat only lettuce and other raw vegetables. Her mother notices and tries to convince her that it's not good for her health to adopt such a drastic diet for the sake of getting thin, but Marilyn doesn't listen.

Then her grandmother sits her down and tells her, "Honey, only dogs like bones. If you look like a bone, you'll just attract dogs." Interestingly, this message resonates with her, so she decides to focus on trying to love who she is.

The Drop Off

At dusk, the orange school bus squealed to a stop along the winding country road. Its doors creaked open, and grown people stepped out—some in pigtails and saddle shoes, others in varsity jackets too tight at the shoulders. They giggled with adult voices, their eyes heavy with years they pretended not to carry.

At each house, strange in its familiarity, children stood waiting in pressed slacks and pearls, sipping from mugs and clutching newspapers like tiny executives. They nodded without speaking as the grown "students" shuffled past them, entering homes that didn't feel like theirs.

The bus pulled away. No one looked back.

Oops

They tumbled across the den floor, bare skin bouncing from the sofa to the loveseat, the July night warm with mischief.

"Stop it!" she gasped, laughing as he tickled her sides.

He grinned, relentless.

"Mercy!" she squealed, squirming—but he didn't. He loved how wild she looked when she surrendered to joy.

Then it happened.

She became silent, her eyes wide with horror. A warmth spread beneath her.

The antique rug—the Persian heirloom his grandfather smuggled home from Cairo—was ruined.

He blinked. She blinked. Then, they burst into laughter.

It shouldn't have been that funny, but it was.

The Library
After Richard Brautigan

Ellison built the library by hand, just past the chapel, near the old train tracks. No system, no catalog—only stories townspeople needed to let go: lost children, hidden crimes, love never spoken aloud. He believed memory deserved a home. Some came to read. Others came to forget. One came to burn.

Before dawn, fire swallowed the shelves, turned secrets to smoke. By sunrise, nothing remained but ash and silence. No one claimed it. No one asked.

Ellison returned with lumber, hands ready. This time, he wrote the first story himself—about a town that feared memory more than fire.

Black and Yellow

After Frank Ocean

The day she died, the sky bloomed pink and white, soft as breath. We scattered her ashes by the shore where she once taught me to float—"Don't fight the water," she'd said, fingers brushing my back like wind through linen.

Now, each tide feels like a memory rising too fast. I hear her in the hush between waves, in the hush between thoughts. Nothing lasts, she warned me, but that doesn't stop me from holding on.

I lie in the surf, sun on my face, letting go inch by inch. The current carries me. I don't need to swim.

THIS USED TO BE OUR PLAYGROUND

AFTER MADONNA

The swings are rusted now, chains sighing in the wind like old voices. This used to be our place—chalk hearts on pavement, secrets traded beneath twilight. She wore braids, I wore bruises from falling too hard for things I couldn't keep. We swore we'd never leave, but time is a thief with soft shoes.

I walk past the field, empty but restless with ghosts. Her laugh still echoes off the bleachers.

The town's smaller now, or maybe I've just grown too big for what it once held.

Still, I linger where everything felt endless, and we were always enough.

BROTHA

IN MEMORY OF ANGIE STONE

They played "Brotha" late that night, after hearing the news, shedding soft tears. He stood beside his wife, her hand tucked into his. The first time he heard that song, they were young, sweating on a summer porch, Angie's voice pouring out the screen door like balm.

He remembered how it made him stand taller, made him feel seen—his struggles, his scars, his slow-won peace. Angie sang to the part of him the world tried to forget.

Now she was gone, and still, her voice wrapped around him.

He squeezed his wife's hand.

"I'm still your brotha," he whispered.

An Alternate Universe

In one of the alternate universes, the classical music foundation is built around the contributions of Joseph Bologne, and there are only rumblings of a German named Wolfgang Amadeus. In this universe, Viola Davis has been nominated for 21 academy awards in her career and is paid top dollar, while Meryl Streep has four nominations and must take to the media to bring attention to the fact she is paid less than Viola, although they have the exact same classical training. Of course, this alternate universe has had 45 Black presidents and only one white president. Protesting is encouraged there.

THE HOROLOGIST

Benjamin spent forty-five years building one watch—each gear filed by hand, each spring tuned like a hymn. It was meant to be perfect, eternal, the kind of timepiece people whispered about long after he was gone.

Now, old and alone, he has finished it. It ticks smoothly, steadily, flawlessly.

He chuckles at the irony. All that time spent mastering time, and he missed so much of it—his son's first steps, his mother's last breath, whole summers lost to silence and metal.

He sets the watch on the mantle, unwound.

For once, he decides, time can keep itself.

The Yearbook

S hawn clutched his blank yearbook tightly, weaving through the halls with a mission: to get Nia to sign it first. Not second. Not squeezed between Jerome and Mrs. Fletcher. *First.*

He wanted her words to breathe, to sprawl like jazz—maybe a heart, maybe "Love," maybe just his name, but written like it *meant* something.

When he asked, she laughed. "You serious?"

He nodded like his life depended on it.

She took the pen, slow and deliberate, and wrote half a page.

Later, he read it repeatedly, each word a melody.

Nia would be the only one to sign it.

OH MERDE!

Maurice taught himself French the way some folks learn to fight—off YouTube and pure emotion. No verbs. No greetings. Just wall-to-wall profanity. By the time he landed in Paris, he could curse like a local, but couldn't order water without offending someone's grandmother.

At a café, he tried to ask for a croissant. The waiter blinked, then backed away slowly.

He called the Eiffel Tower a "metal-ass baguette" and got a thumbs-up from a street performer.

Tourists avoided him. Locals were... *intrigued*.

He didn't see Paris the traditional way, but he sure left his *putain* mark on the city.

Dreams of Atlanta

J ackson found himself in a dream shaped like *Atlanta*—not the city, the show. Streets looped like records, scenes folding into themselves. Darius floated by on a bike made of smoke, whispering, "Time ain't real here, bro."

He followed laughter into a kitchen with no doors. Paper Boi rapped backward on a broken TV. Van danced barefoot in slow motion, her eyes saying *run*, her smile saying *stay*.

Every escape rerouted him back to the beginning—same hallway, same peach.

When his alarm finally broke the spell, he sat up dazed, unsure if he'd woken...or just been written out.

The Filmmaker

Arnold filmed his feature-length movie on a cracked iPhone 13—sunlight, shadows, raw truths stitched together with passion. He edited on his laptop, sound mixed in a closet with blankets for walls.

He sent it out to festivals and streamers.

The rejections came: "Not industry standard." "Lacks polish." No one saw the poetry in pixels, the pain in each frame.

They wanted gloss. He gave them grit.

Undeterred, he uploaded it online. Within days, it spread—no permission, just truth.

The gatekeepers may have shut him out, but the streets knew. And the world, in its own way, was watching.

Part Four
Shade

Dance Challenge

They have been working on the latest TikTok dance challenge for three days and are almost ready to record their version. After two dry runs, they launch into their best attempt at the choreography, and everyone hits her mark on all of the right beats—even Keisha. This will surely be the best version of the dance once it's posted.

When Lana goes to upload the video, she receives an alert on her phone from one of her friends that a new dance challenge is making the rounds.

Lana rounds up her friends in hopes of being faster this time.

FALLING

Every fall, Nate is out there, rake in hand, chasing leaves that never stop coming. The yard mocks him with its quiet apathy. He clears a space, turns, and it's covered again. Even his dreams are filled with rust-colored piles and the soft scrape of tines. His back aches, but it's deeper than that now. Something in him feels loose, untethered. Neighbors wave, then vanish into their homes. The trees, unbothered, let go without looking back.

Some mornings, Nate watches a single leaf fall, slow and aimless, and wonders if he'll drift like that, too: tired, quiet, waiting to land.

Nocturnal Salvation

As the years passed, Quentin found himself sleeping more. Not out of exhaustion, but joy. He collected plush pillows like souvenirs, tested blankets like wine, and wore pajamas softer than memory. Friends joked he was sleeping his life away, but he only smiled, slipping back beneath the covers. In dreams, he walked through cities made of light, heard his mother's laugh again, kissed girls he'd forgotten. Awake felt like the in-between. "Life is but a dream," the old song said, and Quentin believed it. So he let go, gently, night after night, rocking in the cradle of everything he loved.

For Carolyn, From Grandma

When Grandma passed, she left behind a worn leather book, its spine soft like angel kisses. "For Carolyn," the note read, in looping cursive.

Late one night, beneath a blanket of silence, Carolyn opened it. Pages shimmered and pulsed, as the text pulled her through. She landed in a world of lavender skies and moonlit rivers, where trees bowed in recognition. A portrait hung in the crystal hall: Grandma, young, crowned, smiling. Creatures spoke her name with reverence. "She ruled with heart," they said. Carolyn wept, but only a little. The throne stood waiting. The story was still being written.

WHEN A HIATUS BECOMES MORE

He can feel it in his soul: he is near retirement. The irony of it all is that he chose to become a writer because writer's *don't* retire. They simply write until they expire. But these days he is feeling used up, as if his choices have left him nearly depleted. He's written thousands of stories, hundreds of books. He has broken rules and put them back together. He has won awards and not been nominated for others. He is tired. He knows that there are more stories left to write, but he has convinced himself others should write them.

Selective Amnesia

They made love countless times in the shadows of the city, cramped apartments off the train line, but they can't remember each other's names years later. He thinks of it as amnesia from orgasms, but she simply cannot bring herself to remember the name of a person for whom she knew only intimately.

One day she will see him on TV and think to herself, "I knew him once."

He will hear her voice on the radio one day and wonder, "Could that be her?"

It all seems rather pointless in the end, but life can sometimes be that way.

Twisted Fairytales

Little Red Riding Hood is the perfect name for one whose cloak is covered in the blood of a wolf she has slaughtered. In this version, her hood is white, as white as the imaginations that created her, as white as her skin. The wolf is also white (*did you think I'd make him big and brown?*), and this lone wolf has already disemboweled Red's grandmother (*there are few things more horrifying than witnessing the mauling of a loved one.*) Red is left with only one choice: go Liam Neeson on it so that all the blood rains upon her.

A Razor Blade
Named Prince

It was the coldest breakup ever, but only a few of us understood it.

Khari and Portia were standing in the middle of the SUB*, and we were all waiting on it. We knew Portia had a thing for Devon and was going to end things with Khari, so everyone was there. We knew Khari's heartbreak shouldn't have been our entertainment, but there wasn't much going on on campus that day.

Portia ended it by saying, "You're like the bass line to 'When the Doves Cry.' I thought I needed you. Turns out I didn't."

We mourned Khari that day.

---

* Student Union Building

BOOMERANG

Sharice arrived unannounced, a light rap at his door. Outside, rain whispered against the windowpane. When Torrance opened the door, she stood on the threshold—trench coat cinched, eyes burning with heat.

No umbrella or words were needed as her fingers undid each button.

Beneath: nothing but skin and intention.

His breath caught.

"You remember the movie," she whispered, stepping inside.

He could hardly remember the title, but knew the scene. He reached to touch what was once imagined.

The door closed, and the rain kept falling, a soundtrack deep into the night.

Some scenes were meant to be experienced.

The Dude Made Us Dance

After Quincy Jones

D J hadn't danced since his mother passed —too much weight in the music, too many ghosts in the rhythm. But tonight, "Ai No Corrida" blared from the speakers like a dare. His wife grabbed his hand, laughing, barefoot on the cool kitchen tile.

"Come on, baby," she said. "Don't think. Just move."

He hesitated, then stepped into the groove. Horns flared, bass thumped, and suddenly he was twelve again, spinning in the living room, his mother clapping doing her two-step joyfully.

Remembering her smile, he continued to move. In that moment, grief became motion.

He didn't stop dancing until morning.

2 A.M. IN THE HARRIET TUBMAN QUADRANGLE

Alexandra's room glowed dim behind lace curtains, incense curling like memories. "Beauty" by Dru Hill played low on her boombox, worn from too many rewinds.

She sat on her twin bed, knees drawn, reading his letter again—folded in quarters, ink smudged from her thumbs and stray teardrops.

Trevor had dropped out last spring. He'd said that Washington, DC, was pulling at him too hard.

But his words still lived here with her.

You were the softest part of that place, he wrote. *You made it feel like home.*

She pressed the letter to her chest.

Then she pressed rewind.

The Recipe Book

At a yard sale, Kwame found an old binder, thick and worn, held together by love and duct tape. *Recipes* was scribbled on the cover, and inside, there were grease-stained index cards tucked into pockets. He chose the first one, an okra stew with smoked turkey neck.

As the pot simmered, the air shifted.

Suddenly, he was standing in a small Southern kitchen, wooden boards beneath his feet, Nina Simone humming over the radio in the corner. A woman stirred a pot.

"You hungry, baby?"

"Yes, ma'am."

Each bite tasted like home.

He couldn't wait to try the other cards.

<h1 style="text-align:center">A.D. 2025</h1>

AFTER FAT BELLY BELLA

Ralph's name never graced a plaque or street sign. He lived in the spaces between things: his mother's hands over the old wood stove, his sister's laugh echoing in the hallway. No monuments, no buildings—just the quiet persistence of memory.

The city moved on, indifferent to his absence, but it couldn't forget him. He lingered in the things he touched—the warmth of the rain, the coolness of a breeze.

You won't be naming no buildings after me, he thought.

But you'll feel me in the silence. In every single space. In all of the places I left behind.

At the Crossroads of Fame

Their voices once ruled the airwaves, smooth as velvet, filled with aching love and longing. But the story behind their rise was dark—two members gone, swallowed by tragedy, one lost to the poison of fame, another locked away behind bars.

James, the last, lingered in an asylum's quiet halls. His mind cracked, his once golden voice now a broken echo. Whispers circled: had they struck a deal with the devil? No one could say for sure.

But the music lived on, wildly popular, timeless.

And James, alone in his cage, hummed the same tune, trapped between genius and ruin.

A Letter From Your Father

Hey PJ,

I'm writing this because I know time's running out. The streets don't care about me, and I've probably got more time behind me than ahead. I'm sorry I couldn't do better. I should've made different choices, should've fought harder for a better life for you.

I'm never gonna get to hold you, but just know that I wanted to. I dreamed of it—of being the kind of father I never had the chance to be.

If these streets take me, just remember: I loved you before you were even here. And I always will.

Love you, kid.

SELF-PORTRAIT

The things he wishes he could tell his younger self would fill one of Borges's libraries. There is no shortage of embarrassment or shame, mistakes like fan letters to one's worst impulses. But there are things he *did* get right along his journey, things that, at the time, seemed to be arbitrary choices that somehow yielded the most spectacular fruit. He understands that it took the combination of those poor choices, as well as the inadvertent smart choices, to bring him to this present moment. Still, he sees himself like David and Goliath, not unlike the depictions in Caravaggio's painting.

WATERMELON

It bothers Nakia that her son loves watermelon so much. When she was growing up, her mother gave her specific instructions on how (with a fork and a plate) and when (when you're not around white people) to eat watermelon. She wants to pretend that stereotypes are a thing of the past, that Obama was a balm for that, but she knows better. When her son picks up a slice of melon, sprinkles salt on it, and sucks on it, her stomach drops. She wants him to become his own person, but history will not relinquish its hold on her.

APES

Rashad's son wants to go as Donkey Kong for Halloween. This seems like a no-brainer. Rashad grew up playing *Donkey Kong*, *Mario Brothers*, and every game in that narrative family, had raised his son to appreciate gaming by starting off with those games, but something doesn't sit right with him when he thinks about his son wearing a costume of that character. Even though Mario and Luigi are white, he would rather his son goes as one of them instead. It's the ape thing, Rashad knows. He won't voice it aloud, but the stigma of stereotypes is a beast.

CROWDFUNDING MY COUSIN'S CRAZY DREAM

I have to give my cousin credit. He is determined to make his porno. Of course, he doesn't call it that. He hints that there might be some unsimulated acts of a sexual nature in his film. So he's out in these streets crowdfunding. The tentative title? *Soylent Ass*. Now, I'm no film aficionado, but he says it's based on a film where (spoiler alert) people are eating people! So I'm like, "You doing some cannibalism stuff?" And he says, "No, my characters aren't eating people. Thus the title."

If you get an email from my cousin, just ignore it.

Editing the Collection

Irene read through the short story collection slowly, carefully.

"What do you think?" Martin finally asked.

She paused, considering her phrasing. "It's good—but it's a little uneven."

"Uneven?"

"Yes. Some pieces read like poetry, while others are a little crude. I don't know what you're going for here."

"So you're saying if I take out the crowd-funding story, the letter from the father, and the two pieces about stereotypes, it would read better?"

"You said it, not me."

"You think the watermelon and ape stories are redundant."

"Just a little."

Martin didn't doubt Irene, but he kept them anyway.

BLACK BOY IN FLIGHT

I am your Black boy in flight story, the story where he falls in love and finds himself lifting towards the sky, as if he had a cape and goggles like Flyboy, as if he had wings and goggles like Sam Wilson. In this version, he has just had his first kiss on the steps of Harkness Hall, where Spike's Gammas pledged in '87. Originally, he had spotted her on Brawley Drive and offered to carry her books. After some Popeye's and an engaging conversation as they walked back to campus, it happened.

Now, he is flying off these pages.

Purple

Toni's father gave her the book as a gift. He'd seen it on one of the tables at the local bookstore. He even joked about the fact that their last name was the same as the author's.

"Guess our plantation owners were related, huh?" he said, as if this was the first time he'd ever made that joke.

Still, the book intrigued her, its beautiful purple color, the book's title in a large font across the cover. She'd never seen either film adaptation or play, but she was curious to read it, to know what made this book so special.

RAKIM'S JOINT

I only mean to love her, even in silences. Morning creeps in, soft and blue, through the blinds of our walk-up. She's still dreaming, limbs tangled in thrifted sheets, vinyl skipping somewhere in the kitchen—D'Angelo, maybe. I roll a joint with the same care I use to touch her, then light it, exhaling slow thoughts. My sketchbook waits by the window, half-full of lines that look like her laugh. This city hums with chaos, but she moves like stillness. I don't say forever, but I stay. Not because I have to, but because in this moment, we are one.

Robyn's Joint

I only mean to love him, even in the in-betweens. Morning fog curls through the fire escape, sweet with smoke and jasmine. My thrifted robe slides off one shoulder as I sip coffee from a chipped mug, Miles playing softly. I write poems on receipts and lose them in coat pockets, like prayers I never meant to keep. He's still asleep, mouth open like trust. I think about kissing him, or maybe leaving a note. I think about forever, but only in lowercase. This city doesn't promise permanence, just possibility—and I'm learning to love things that don't last.

Ran Walker in the Afroverse

Ran sits at his desk, writing a 100-word story about Ran Walker writing a 100-word story about Ran Walker writing a 100-word story. The air hums. The clock ticks backward. In the story, Ran types the same line, over and over, watching the words fold into themselves like origami dreams. Each version of him wonders if he's the first, or just another page in a book that never ends. He writes to escape, but the story keeps closing in. Ninety-eight. Ninety-nine. One hundred. He hits save, but the file disappears. Outside, it's still night. Or maybe it always has been.

ACKNOWLEDGMENTS

Thank you to Lauren and Zoë, my family and friends, my colleagues and fellow writers.

All stories in this collection are original and have never been published elsewhere.

About the Author
In 100 Words

Ran Walker (he/him) is the author of over 40 books. His short stories, flash fiction, microfiction, and poetry have appeared in a variety of anthologies and journals.

He is the winner of the Indie Author Project's National Indie Author of the Year Award, the Black Caucus of the American Library Association Best Fiction Ebook Award, the Virginia Indie Author Project Award for Adult Fiction, and the Blind Corner Afrofuturism Microfiction Contest. Ran is an Associate Professor of English and Creative Writing at Hampton University and teaches with Writer's Digest University. He lives in Virginia with his wife and daughter.

ALSO BY RAN WALKER

B-Sides and Remixes

30 Love: A Novel

Mojo's Guitar: A Novel/(Il était une fois Morris Jones)

Afro Nerd in Love: A Novella

The Keys of My Soul: A Novel

The Race of Races: A Novel

The Illest: A Novella

Bessie, Bop, or Bach: Collected Stories

Four Floors (with Sabin Prentis)

Black Hand Side: Stories

White Pages: A Novel

She Lives in My Lap

Reverb

Work-In-Progress

Daykeeper

Most of My Heroes Don't Appear On No Stamps

Portable Black Magic: Tales of the Afro Strange

The Strange Museum: 50-Word Stories

Bees + Things + Flowers: Microfictions

The World Is Yours: Microfictions

Can I Kick It?: Sneaker Microfiction and Poetry (with Van Garrett)

The Golden Book: A 50-Year Marriage Told In 50-Word Stories

Keep It 100: 100-Word Stories

A Burst of Gray: A Novel In 100-Word Stories

The Library of Afro Curiosities: 100-Word Stories

Black Marker: A Novel in 100-Word Stories

GloKat and the Art of Timing: A Novel in 100-Word Stories

A Different Kind of Christmas Story: A Carol in 100-Word Stories

Spaceships Don't Come Equipped with Rearview Mirrors: 50-Word Stories

This Is Not a Poem/Story: 100-Word Stories

Parts of Speech: 100-Word Stories

Four Suits: A Deck of 100-Word Stories

O'ahu: Prose Poems

Apollo's Toy Box

Gods Among Men

One Hundred Ways: A Handbook for Writing 100-Word Stories

Sneaker Marauders: Poems (with Van G. Garrett)

The Night Before the End of the World

Fragments of the Afroverse: 100-Word Stories

Deux: A 50 x 50 Micro Novella

www.ingramcontent.com/pod-product-compliance
Lightning Source LLC
Chambersburg PA
CBHW040909010826

48978CB00013BB/1211